Franky
The Finicky Flamingo

By

Wanda

ISBN 978-0-9981958-2-7
Library of Congress - 2017915722
For more infromation about this book or other books or to contact Wanda Luthman please visit
wandalu64@gmail.com
www.wandaluthman.wordpress.com
www.facebook.com/wluthman

Franky, the finicky flamingo
Is perfectly pink from head to toe.
A black bowtie adorns his neck
And he preens himself with a peckity-peck.

He balances himself upon one foot
And sings a song, "No sooty-soot!"
He sleeps with his head tucked under his wing.
But, there is just one little thing...

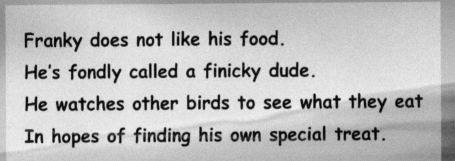

Franky does not like his food.

He's fondly called a finicky dude.

He watches other birds to see what they eat

In hopes of finding his own special treat.

A robin gobbles a wiggly worm.

But, those just make Franky's stomach squirm.

A blue jay loves a crunchy nut.
But, that gets stuck in Franky's gut.

A hummingbird sips sweet nectar.

But, Franky gets fuzzy from all the sugar.

A golden finch picks brown thistle.

But, that makes Franky's tummy bristle.

Franky stands still, with eyes so wide.
Something feels tickly and strange inside.

Franky's bright pink begins to fade.

And soon becomes a fainter shade.

This makes him worry. He starts to cry,

"My color is fading, oh my, oh my!"

An owl swoops to his rescue.

Speaking words of advice that are wise and true.

"You need pink shellfish to eat. It's clear!

That is just what you need, my dear."

Franky thanks the owl for her help.
And munches on shrimp in the nearby kelp.
"Yum, yum," he says, "this tastes delicious."
Owl doesn't mention it's also nutritious.

Then, Franky's skin brightens in a blinkety-blink.
He's back to his favorite shade of pink.
Franky wasn't finicky for no reason, you see.
He needed pink food, so pink he could be!

He smiles and rubs his satisfied tummy
And will search tomorrow for more things yummy.
Then, Franky discovers all sorts of pink foods
That are just right for finicky dudes.

"Now that I'm back to my favorite pink,
What in the world am I going to drink?"

CPSIA information can be obtained
at www.ICGtesting.com
Printed in the USA
BVHW09s0958310818
526000BV00021B/187/P